S0-BRG-718

Explore the Continents

Where on Earth are
Rivers?

DISCARD

Bobbie Kalman

Crabtree Publishing Company

www.crabtreebooks.com

Public Library
Incorporated 1862
Barrie, Ontario

Explore the Continents

Created by Bobbie Kalman

For my cousin Miki Halasz, who is totally amazing, with lots of love from Bobbie, Peter, and Samantha

Author and Editor-in-Chief
Bobbie Kalman

Editor
Kathy Middleton

Proofreader
Crystal Sikkens

Photo research
Bobbie Kalman

Design
Bobbie Kalman
Katherine Berti

Prepress technician
Katherine Berti

Print and production coordinator
Margaret Amy Salter

Illustrations
Barbara Bedell: pages 4 (frog)
Katherine Berti: pages 6–7, 27 (crocodile)
Robert MacGregor: page 20
Jeannette McNaughton-Julich: pages 4 (dolphins), 5
Margaret Amy Salter: page 4 (goldfish)

Photographs
Dreamstime: George Politsarnov: page 22 (bottom)
Dziewul/Shutterstock: page 9 (top right)
Thinkstock: pages 21 (top right), 22–23 (background),
 24–25 (background)
All other images by Shutterstock

Library and Archives Canada Cataloguing in Publication

Kalman, Bobbie, author
 Where on Earth are rivers? / Bobbie Kalman.

(Explore the continents)
Includes index.
Issued in print and electronic formats.
ISBN 978-0-7787-0502-4 (bound).--ISBN 978-0-7787-0506-2 (pbk.).--
ISBN 978-1-4271-8231-9 (pdf).--ISBN 978-1-4271-8227-2 (html)

 1. Rivers--Juvenile literature. I. Title. II. Series: Explore the
continents

GB1203.8.K35 2014   j551.48   C2014-900892-9
                                                        C2014-900893-7

Library of Congress Cataloging-in-Publication Data

Kalman, Bobbie.
 Where on earth are rivers? / Bobbie Kalman.
  pages cm. -- (Explore the continents)
 Includes index.
 ISBN 978-0-7787-0502-4 (reinforced library binding) -- ISBN
978-0-7787-0506-2 (paperback) -- ISBN 978-1-4271-8231-9
(electronic-pdf) -- ISBN 978-1-4271-8227-2 (electronic-html)
 1. Rivers--Juvenile literature. I. Title.

 GB1203.8.K354 2014
 910.916'93--dc23

                                            2014004891

Crabtree Publishing Company
www.crabtreebooks.com   1-800-387-7650

Printed in the USA/052014/SN20140313

Copyright © **2014 CRABTREE PUBLISHING COMPANY**. All rights reserved. No part of this publication may be reproduced, stored in a retrieval system or be transmitted in any form or by any means, electronic, mechanical, photocopying, recording, or otherwise, without the prior written permission of Crabtree Publishing Company. In Canada: We acknowledge the financial support of the Government of Canada through the Canada Book Fund for our publishing activities.

Published in Canada
Crabtree Publishing
616 Welland Ave.
St. Catharines, Ontario
L2M 5V6

Published in the United States
Crabtree Publishing
PMB 59051
350 Fifth Avenue, 59th Floor
New York, New York 10118

Published in the United Kingdom
Crabtree Publishing
Maritime House
Basin Road North, Hove
BN41 1WR

Published in Australia
Crabtree Publishing
3 Charles Street
Coburg North
VIC 3058

DISCARDED

Contents

Rivers on continents 4

Water on Earth 6

Learning about rivers 8

Longest and largest 10

North American rivers 12

South American rivers 14

The Amazon River 16

Rivers in Asia 18

Asian river mouths 20

Rivers in Europe 22

Cities by rivers 24

The rivers of Africa 26

Australia and Oceania 28

Why we need rivers 30

Glossary and Index 32

Rivers on continents

Rivers can be found on six of Earth's seven **continents**. Continents are huge areas of land. From largest to smallest, the seven continents are Asia, Africa, North America, South America, Antarctica, Europe, and Australia/Oceania. Antarctica has no rivers.

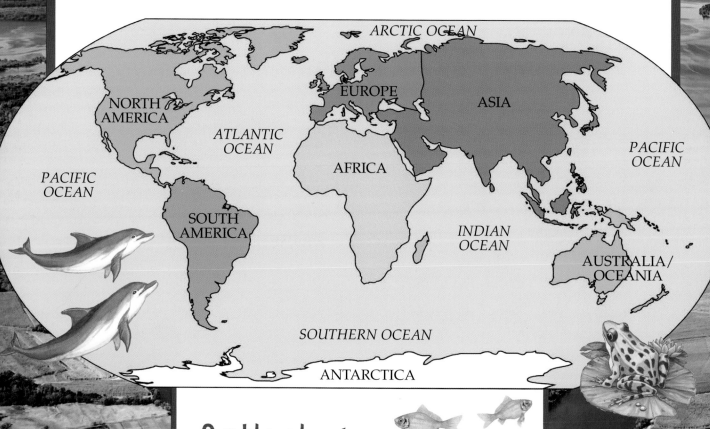

Our blue planet

Water covers about three-quarters of Earth. Huge areas of water are called **oceans**. Many rivers end at oceans.

ocean

river

Oceans and seas

The five oceans on Earth flow around the seven continents. The oceans, from largest to smallest, are the Pacific Ocean, Atlantic Ocean, Indian Ocean, Southern Ocean, and Arctic Ocean. The Pacific Ocean is named twice on the map because it is so large that it covers almost half of Earth.

Water on Earth

A **river** is a body of water that moves from one place to another. The **source** of a river is where it begins. Many rivers start on mountains and flow down to lower places. The **mouth** of a river is where it ends. Many rivers flow into oceans. Some flow into lakes or other rivers.

Moving and changing

Rivers change as they flow from source to mouth. They drop quickly down mountains and wind slowly over the land in **meanders**, or large curves. As rivers move, they shape the land.

The rocks carried by flowing water bounce and bump along the sides and bottoms of rivers. They break off pieces of land and change the landscape.

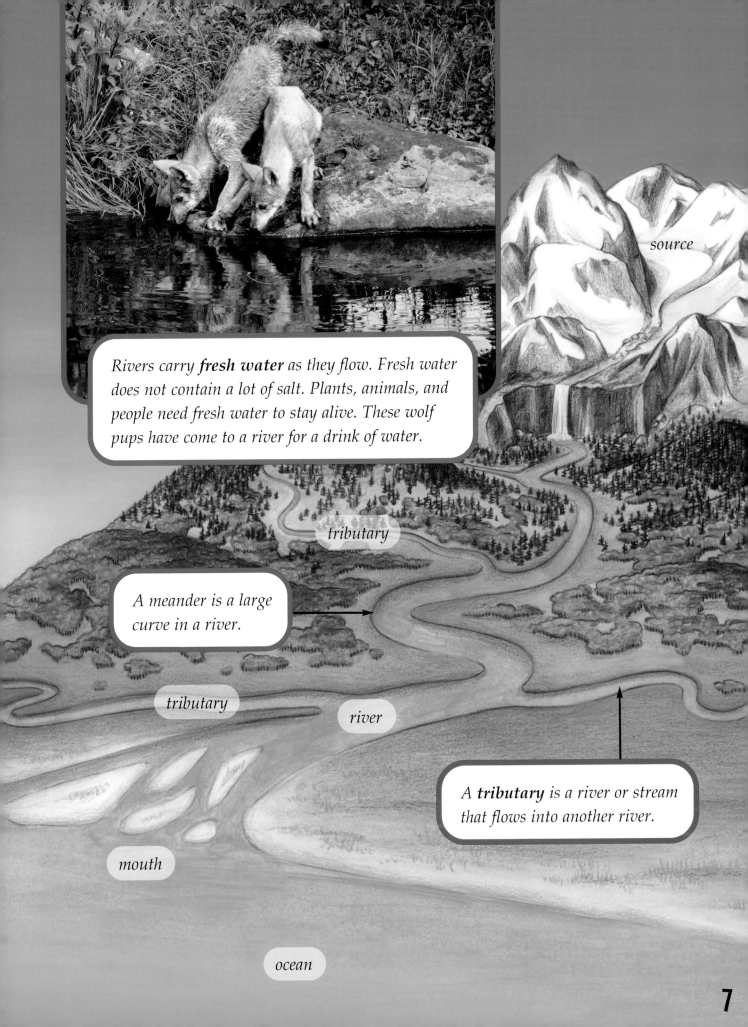

source

Rivers carry **fresh water** as they flow. Fresh water does not contain a lot of salt. Plants, animals, and people need fresh water to stay alive. These wolf pups have come to a river for a drink of water.

tributary

A meander is a large curve in a river.

tributary

river

A **tributary** is a river or stream that flows into another river.

mouth

ocean

Learning about rivers

Some important river words, such as source, mouth, tributary, and meander, were introduced on pages 6 and 7. These pages will give you some other important words and information about rivers.

Banks are the sides of rivers. Water flows between riverbanks. These deer are standing on the bank of a river.

A **canal** is a human-made waterway. This canal is in Venice, Italy. Italy is a country in Europe.

A **delta** is a large triangular area at the mouth of a river, where the river splits into slow-flowing **channels**.

channels

An **estuary** is where a river meets an ocean. Fresh water from the river mixes with salt water from the ocean.

ocean

estuary

river

glacier

river

Rapids are shallow, rocky parts of rivers where the *currents* are very strong and fast. A current is the movement of water in a certain direction.

A *riverbed* is the bottom of a river. This manatee is swimming along a riverbed.

A *glacier* is a huge, slow-moving body of ice. When glaciers melt, water runs down mountains as rivers.

A *drainage basin* is an area of land where water from rain or snow collects and drains into a river.

A *waterfall* is a sudden drop in a river as it flows over a rock cliff.

Longest and largest

The map below shows some of Earth's longest rivers. The three longest rivers are located on three different continents. The Nile River is in Africa. It is the longest at 4,160 miles (6,695 km). The second-longest river, and largest, is the Amazon River in South America. It is 4,049 miles (6,516 km) long. The third-longest river, the Yangtze River, is in Asia. It is 3,964 miles (6,380 km) long. Find these rivers on the map below. If you cannot remember the names of the continents or oceans, learn them on page 4.

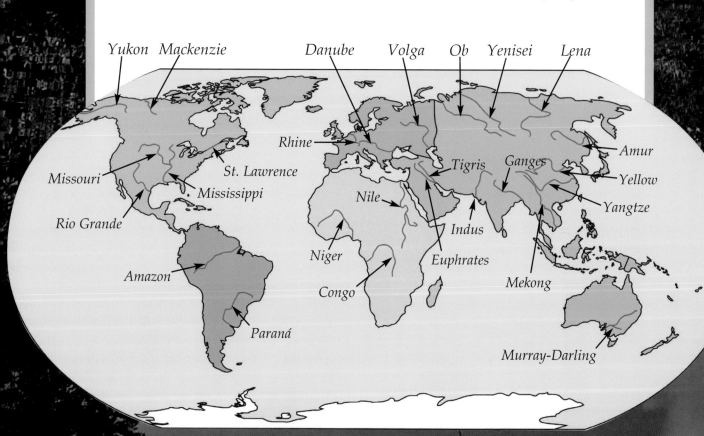

The Amazon River is not the longest river on Earth, but it is the largest. It carries more water than any other river. The large picture on these pages shows the Amazon River (also see pages 16–17).

The Nile River flows through eleven countries in Africa. Its mouth is at the Mediterranean Sea. The Nile flows through Cairo, the capital city of Egypt. Learn more about the rivers in Africa on pages 26-27.

North American rivers

There are hundreds of rivers in North America. The Missouri River is the longest. It is a tributary of the Mississippi River, the second-longest river. The St. Lawrence River is another very important waterway. It connects the Great Lakes in Canada and the United States with the Atlantic Ocean. The Great Lakes hold about one-fifth of Earth's fresh water.

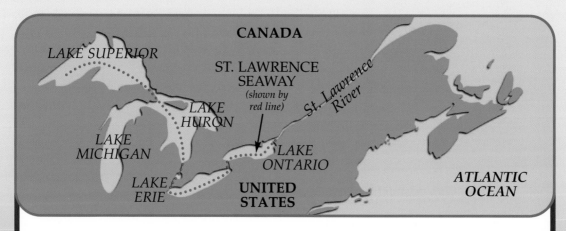

The St. Lawrence Seaway and the Great Lakes

The lakes that make up the Great Lakes are Lake Superior, Lake Huron, Lake Erie, Lake Ontario, and Lake Michigan. Four of the lakes are on the border of Canada and the United States. Lake Michigan is only in the United States. The Great Lakes are connected to one another by rivers and canals. Canals are human-made waterways. The St. Lawrence Seaway is the name of the system of canals that connects the Great Lakes to the Atlantic Ocean.

The Missouri River joins the Mississippi River at St. Louis, Missouri, located near the midpoint of the Mississippi River. Its Gateway Arch honors St. Louis as the Gateway to the West. The arch is the tallest monument in the United States.

Gateway Arch

Niagara Falls includes three waterfalls on the border of Canada and the United States. Horseshoe Falls in Canada, shown here, is the largest. The American Falls and Bridal Veil Falls are in the United States. All three falls are part of the Niagara River, which ends at Lake Ontario in Canada.

South American rivers

The continent of South America lies between two oceans. The Pacific Ocean is on its west coast, and the Atlantic Ocean is on its east **coast**. The **equator** passes through the top part of South America. The weather is hot and rainy in the areas close to the equator. The Amazon River is located there. The Amazon River is South America's longest river, and the Paraná River is the second-longest. Other important rivers are the Negro, Uruguay, and Madeira.

*The Puerto Madero Waterfront is a district of Buenos Aires, the **capital** of Argentina. It occupies a large part of the Río de la Plata riverbank. The Río de la Plata is an estuary in which fresh water and sea water mix. The fresh water comes from the Paraná River and the Uruguay River. The salt water comes from the Atlantic Ocean.*

The Iguaçu River, an important tributary of the Paraná River, flows through Brazil and Argentina. Iguaçu Falls lie along the Iguaçu River. The falls are in the north of Argentina, on the border with Brazil. The horseshoe-shaped falls are made up of 275 waterfalls. They are more than twice as wide as Niagara Falls.

The Amazon River

The Amazon River is the second-longest river in the world and the largest river because it carries the most water. It contains one-fifth of Earth's fresh water. Thousands of tributaries flow into the Amazon. The river is so wide that many people call it a "river sea." The source of the Amazon River is high in the Andes Mountains of Peru. The Amazon River flows through the Amazon Rainforest, the world's largest **tropical rain forest**. This huge forest is home to many kinds of plants and millions of **species**, or types, of animals, including birds, monkeys, caimans, frogs, and jaguars.

poison dart frog

parrot

squirrel monkey

caiman

jaguar

The tributary Rio Negro joins the Amazon at Manaus, Brazil. Manaus is in the middle of the Amazon Rainforest. The only way to reach this city is by plane or boat.

Amazon water lily

Amazon River dolphin

The huge plants in the large picture are Amazon water lilies, the biggest water lilies in the world. They grow in the Amazon River.

Most dolphins live in salt water, but the Amazon River dolphin is a freshwater dolphin. It is also called pink dolphin because its skin looks pink.

The fish above is a piranha. It lives in the Amazon River. It has very sharp teeth!

Rivers in Asia

Asia is the biggest continent, with 50 countries and hundreds of rivers. Earth's third-longest river, the Yangtze River is in Asia. It runs through China and Tibet. The Yellow River, or Huang He, is the third-longest river in Asia. The first Chinese people lived along this river. Other important rivers are the Mekong River in Southeast Asia, the Euphrates and Tigris rivers in Western Asia, the Lena, Ob, and Yenisei rivers in Russia, the Indus River in Pakistan, and the Ganges River in India.

The source of the Ganges River is in the Himalayas, Earth's highest mountains. The river then flows through India and into Bangladesh. Millions of people depend on this river for water. People of the Hindu religion consider Ganges a sacred river.

The Euphrates and Tigris rivers start in the mountains of Turkey. They flow along separate **courses**, or paths, until they meet near the Persian Gulf, which is part of the Indian Ocean.

The Indus River is Pakistan's most important river. The source of this river is in Tibet, and its mouth is the Arabian Sea. The Arabian Sea is part of the Indian Ocean.

In China, the Yangtze River is called **Chang Jiang**, which means long river. It provides the Chinese people with fresh water for drinking and growing crops, fish to eat, transportation, and electricity.

Asian river mouths

Many rivers have their mouths at oceans or at **seas**. Seas are part of oceans. Three oceans that touch Asia are the Arctic Ocean, the Pacific Ocean, and the Indian Ocean. The South China Sea, East China Sea, Philippine Sea, and Sea of Japan are all part of the Pacific Ocean. Some rivers empty into lakes. Follow the rivers on this globe and write down into which ocean, sea, or lake each one drains.

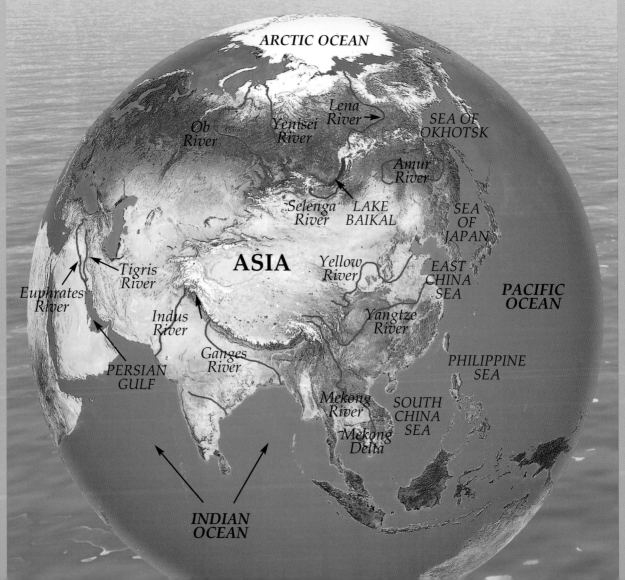

The Lena River is one of three large rivers in Siberia, Russia, that flow into the Arctic Ocean. It is the sixth-longest river in Asia and the eleventh-longest river in the world.

Some river mouths are at lakes. About 330 rivers drain into Lake Baikal in Siberia, Russia. The largest is the Selenga River. Lake Baikal is Earth's oldest lake with the most fresh water.

The Mekong River starts in Tibet and runs through China and several other countries in Asia. It empties into the South China Sea. The Mekong Delta, shown here, is where the Mekong River empties into the sea through a number of tributaries. The delta makes up a large part of the country of Vietnam.

Rivers in Europe

There are many rivers in Europe. The longest is the Volga River in Russia. It is also Europe's largest river. The second-longest river is the Danube. It flows through ten countries and some of Europe's most beautiful cities, such as Budapest and Vienna. Another famous river is the Seine, France's second-longest river.

Volga River

Severn River

Thames River

Oka River

Rhine River

Seine River

Loire River

Danube River

Arno River

The Volga River is 2,193 miles (3,530 km) long. It is in Russia, a country that lies both in Asia and Europe. The Volga River meets another Russian river, the Oka River, at a city called Nizhny Novgorod.

Volga River

Oka River

The Seine River flows through Paris, in France, with many beautiful buildings and structures along its banks, including the Eiffel Tower, shown left.

The Danube River flows for 1,770 miles (2,850 km), passing through the countries of Romania, Serbia, Austria, Germany, Bulgaria, Slovakia, Croatia, Moldova, Ukraine, and Hungary. In Budapest, Hungary, the banks of the Danube River, along with many historic buildings, such as the Parliament building shown here, have been listed as a **World Heritage Site**.

Budapest Parliament building

Cities by rivers

More than 735 million people live in Europe, and most of them live in cities. Many cities, such as Paris, Budapest, Heidelberg, London, and Florence are built on the banks of rivers. Rivers provide people with water and electricity, and they make the landscape of cities more beautiful! Some famous European rivers are the Danube, Rhine, Loire, and Thames. The river in the large picture on these pages is the Arno River in Florence, Italy.

The Rhine River starts in the mountains of Switzerland and flows through Austria, Germany, Belgium, Luxembourg, France, and the Netherlands, where it ends at the North Sea. The city shown here is Heidelberg, Germany.

The Loire River is France's longest river. Many castles were built along its banks. This castle is in the city of Amboise.

The longest river in the United Kingdom is the Severn River. The second-longest is the Thames River, shown here, which flows through London, England.

The rivers of Africa

Africa is the second-largest continent, with more than 50 countries. The longest river on Earth, the Nile, flows through Africa. The Congo River is the world's deepest river and the second-largest by the amount of water it carries. The Niger River, the third-longest river in Africa, flows through the western part of the continent. Victoria Falls, the largest waterfall on Earth is also in Africa. It is on the Zambezi River in southern Africa. The large picture on these pages shows Victoria Falls.

Nile River

Niger River

AFRICA

Congo River

Zambezi River

Victoria Falls

Victoria Falls is twice as high and wide as Niagara Falls in North America.

Many kinds of animals live in and along the rivers of Africa. These elephants are drinking water in a river. They are also using the water to bathe and cool themselves. Other African animals that visit rivers are lions, wildebeest, cheetahs, and zebras. Hippos and crocodiles live in African rivers.

crocodile

wildebeest

Australia and Oceania

Australia is the smallest continent on Earth. It is completely surrounded by water. Australia is part of a large area called Oceania, which includes New Zealand and many other islands. Australia has among the lowest rainfalls of all the continents because of its hot climate. There are very few rivers and lakes in Australia that have water in them year-long. The longest rivers are the Murray River and the Darling River. Shorter rivers, such as the Yarra River in Melbourne, are important for transportation and as sources of drinking water and electricity.

The Yarra River is 150 miles (242 km) long and has more than 50 tributaries. Although it is not very long, the Yarra River is very important. The city of Melbourne was built on its banks. The river supplies the people of Melbourne with their drinking water.

Rivers in New Zealand

The longest river in New Zealand is the Waikato River with a length of 264 miles (425 km). The largest river with the most water is the Clutha River, shown here, where a **gold rush** took place in the 1860s.

AUSTRALIA

Darling River

WELLINGTON•

Murray River

MELBOURNE•

Yarra River

Waikato River

TASMAN SEA

NORTH ISLAND

NEW ZEALAND

SOUTH ISLAND

PACIFIC OCEAN

Clutha River

Why we need rivers

Without water, there would be no life on Earth. Rivers supply fresh water to plants, animals, and people. We use water for drinking, preparing food, and washing ourselves, our clothes, and our homes. Farmers use water from rivers to **irrigate** their **crops**. Many people catch fish to eat in rivers. Rivers are also used to make electricity. People travel and carry goods on rivers. They also use rivers for **recreational** activities, such as swimming, boating, and kayaking, as this father and son are doing.

Some animals live in rivers, and those that live on land also need rivers. Like this red fox and her pup, they come to drink fresh water. Plants also grow in and around rivers.

Saving water

There is very little fresh water on Earth, so we need to use it wisely. What can you do to save water?

- Turn the water off while you brush your teeth.
- Instead of baths, take showers that are less than five minutes long.
- Save water from your baths or showers to water your plants.
- Share your knowledge about how to save water with your friends.

Learn more ways to save water at: *www.thewaterpage.com/ water-conservation-kids.htm*

Glossary

Note: Some boldfaced words are defined where they appear in the book.

capital The most important city in a country or region, where the government is located

channel A small, thin body of water that connects larger bodies of water

coast Land that is beside an ocean

crops Plants that are grown as foods

equator An imaginary line around the center of Earth, where it is hot all year

gold rush A quick movement of people to an area where gold was found

irrigate To bring water to land or crops through pipes or canals

recreational Describing an activity that is done for fun

species A group of plants or animals that share similar characteristics

tropical rain forest A forest near the equator that receives a lot of rain

World Heritage Site A natural or human-made area or structure, such as a river, forest, waterfall, or building, which is recognized worldwide as important and has special protection

Index

Amazon River 10, 14, 16–17
canals 8, 12
Congo River 26
continents 4–5, 10, 18, 26, 28
Danube River 22, 23, 24
Euphrates River 18, 19
fresh water 7, 8, 14, 16, 17, 19, 21, 30, 31
Ganges River 18
Great Lakes 12
Iguaçu River 15
Indus River 19
lakes 6, 12, 13, 20, 21
Loire River 24, 25
Mekong River 18, 21
Mississippi River 12, 13
Missouri River 12, 13
mountains 6, 9, 16, 18, 19, 24
mouth 6, 8, 11, 19, 20
Negro River 14, 17
Niger River 26
Nile River 10, 26
oceans 4, 5, 6, 8, 10, 12, 14, 18, 19, 20, 21
Paraná River 14
Rhine River 24
seas 5, 11, 19, 20, 21, 24
Seine River 22, 23
source 6, 8, 16, 18, 19
St. Lawrence River 12
Thames River 24, 25
Tigris River 18, 19
tributaries 7, 8, 12, 15, 16, 17, 21, 28
Uruguay River 14
waterfalls 9, 13, 15, 26
Yangtze River 10, 18, 19
Yarra River 28
Yellow River 18